1 3 5 7 9 10 8 6 4 2

Text and illustrations © Ann and Reg Cartwright

Ann and Reg Cartwright have asserted their rights under the Copyright,
Designs and Patents Act, 1988
to be identified as authors and illustrators of this work

First published in the United Kingdom 1989
by Hutchinson Children's Books
First published in Mini Treasures edition 1996
by Red Fox
Random House, 20 Vauxhall Bridge Road, London SW1V 2SA

Random House Australia (Pty) Limited
20 Alfred Street, Milsons Point, Sydney,
New South Wales 2061, Australia

Random House New Zealand Limited
18 Poland Road, Glenfield,
Auckland 10, New Zealand

Random House South Africa (Pty) Limited
PO Box 2263, Rosebank 2121, South Africa

Random House UK Limited Reg. No. 954009

A CIP catalogue record for this book
is available from the British Library

ISBN 009 9725 819

Printed in Singapore

ANN & REG CARTWRIGHT

The Winter Hedgehog

Mini Treasures

RED FOX

One cold, misty autumn afternoon, the hedgehogs gathered in the wood. They were preparing for the long sleep of winter.

All that is, except the smallest hedgehog. 'What is winter?' he had asked his mother.

'Winter comes when we are asleep,' she had replied. 'It can be beautiful, but it can also be dangerous, cruel and very, very cold. It's not for the likes of us. Now go to sleep.'

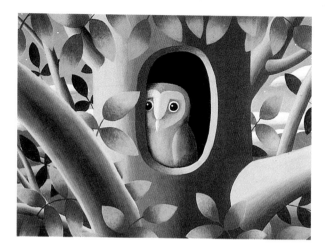

But the smallest hedgehog couldn't sleep.
As evening fell he slipped away to look for
winter. When hedgehogs are determined
they can move very swiftly, and soon the
little hedgehog was far from home. An owl
swooped down from high in a tree.

'Hurry home,' he called. 'It's time for
your long sleep.' But on and on went the
smallest hedgehog until the sky turned dark
and the trees were nothing but shadows.

The next morning, the hedgehog awoke to find the countryside covered in fog. 'Who goes there?' called a voice, and a large rabbit emerged from the mist.

'I'm looking for winter,' replied the hedgehog. 'Can you tell me where it is?'

'Hurry home,' said the rabbit. 'Winter is on its way and it's no time for hedgehogs.'

But the smallest hedgehog wouldn't listen. He was determined to find winter.

Days passed. The little hedgehog found plenty of slugs and insects to eat, but he couldn't find winter anywhere.

Then one day the air turned icy cold. Birds flew home to their roosts and the animals hid in their burrows and warrens. The smallest hedgehog felt very lonely and afraid and wished he was asleep with the other hedgehogs. But it was too late to turn back now.

That night winter came. A frosty wind swept through the grass and blew the last straggling leaves from the trees. In the morning the whole countryside was covered in a carpet of snow.

'Winter!' cried the smallest hedgehog. 'I've found it at last.' And all the birds flew down from the trees to join him.

The trees were completely bare and the snow sparkled on the grass. The little hedgehog went to the river to drink, but it was frozen. He shivered, shook his prickles and stepped on to the ice. His feet began to slide and the faster he scurried, the faster he sped across it. 'Winter is wonderful,' he cried. At first he did not see the fox, like a dark shadow, slinking towards him.

'Hello! Come and join me,' he called as the fox reached the riverbank. But the fox only heard the rumble of his empty belly. With one leap he pounced on to the ice. When the little hedgehog saw his sly yellow eyes he understood what the fox was about. He curled into a ball and spiked his prickles.

'Ouch!' cried the fox. The sharp prickles stabbed his paws and he reeled towards the centre of the river where he disappeared beneath the ice.

'That was close,' the smallest hedgehog cried to himself. 'Winter is beautiful, but it is also cruel, dangerous and very, very cold.'

Colder and colder it grew until the snow
froze under the hedgehog's feet. The snow
came again and a cruel north wind picked
it up and whipped it into a blizzard.
'Winter is dangerous and cruel and very,
very cold,' moaned the little hedgehog.

Luck saved him. A hare scurrying home
gave him shelter in his burrow. By morning
the snow was still falling, but gently now,
covering everything in a soft white blanket.

The smallest hedgehog was enchanted as he watched the pattern his paws made. Reaching the top of a hill, he rolled into a ball and spun over and over, turning himself into a great white snowball as he went. Down and down he rolled until he reached the feet of two children building a snowman.

'Hey, look at this,' said the little girl. 'A perfect head for our snowman.'

'I'm a hedgehog,' he cried. But no one heard his tiny hedgehog voice.

The girl placed the hedgehog snowball on the snowman's body and the boy used a carrot for a nose and pebbles for the eyes.

When the children had gone, the cold and hungry hedgehog nibbled at the carrot nose. As he munched the sun came out and the snow began to melt. He blinked in the bright sunlight, tumbled down the snowman's body and was free.

Time went on.
The hedgehog
saw the world in
its winter cloak.
He saw red
berries disappear
from the hedgerows as
the birds collected them for their winter
larders. And he watched children speed
down the hill on their sleighs.

The winter passed. One day the air grew
warmer and the river began to flow again.
The little hedgehog found crocuses and
snowdrops beneath the trees and he knew
it was time to go home. Slowly he made his
way back to the wood.

From out of every log, sleepy hedgehogs were emerging from their long sleep.

'Where have you been?' they called to him.

'I found winter,' he replied.

'And what was it like?' asked his mother.

'It was beautiful, but it was also...'

'Dangerous, cruel and very, very cold,' finished his mother.

But she was answered by a yawn, a sigh and a snore, and the smallest hedgehog was fast asleep.